WELCOME TO THE ZOO

TICKETS

alison jay

dial books for young readers

DIAL BOOKS FOR YOUNG READERS

A division of Penguin Young Readers Group

Published by The Penguin Group

Penguin Group (USA) Inc., 375 Hudson Street, New York, NY 10014, U.S.A.

Penguin Group (Canada), 90 Eglinton Avenue East, Suite 700, Toronto, Ontario, Canada M4P 2Y3 (a division of Pearson Penguin Canada Inc.)

Penguin Books Ltd, 80 Strand, London WC2R 0RL, England

Penguin Ireland, 25 St. Stephen's Green, Dublin 2, Ireland (a division of Penguin Books Ltd)

Penguin Group (Australia), 250 Camberwell Road, Camberwell, Victoria 3124, Australia (a division of Pearson Australia Group Pty Ltd)

Penguin Books India Pvt Ltd, 11 Community Centre, Panchsheel Park, New Delhi - 110 017, India

Penguin Group (NZ), 67 Apollo Drive, Rosedale, North Shore 0632, New Zealand (a division of Pearson New Zealand Ltd)

Penguin Books (South Africa) (Pty) Ltd, 24 Sturdee Avenue, Rosebank, Johannesburg 2196, South Africa

Penguin Books Ltd, Registered Offices: 80 Strand, London WC2R 0RL, England

Designed by Lily Malcom

Manufactured in China on acid-free paper

Special Markets ISBN 978-0-8037-3422-7 Not for Resale

Library of Congress Cataloging-in-Publication Data is available upon request.

The art was created using alkyd oil paint on paper with crackling varnish.

1 3 5 7 9 10 8 6 4 2

This Imagination Library edition is published by Penguin Group (USA), a Pearson company, exclusively for Dolly Parton's Imagination Library, a not-for-profit program designed to inspire a love of reading and learning, sponsored in part by The Dollywood Foundation. Penguin's trade editions of this work are available wherever books are sold.

*This book is dedicated to
my dear dad, John Stewart Rivers,
whose creativity, ingenuity, and wonderful
sense of humor will inspire me forever.
1930–2007*

Now that you've walked through the zoo, can you find . . . ?

Hint: look for the elephant!

3 of these . . .

15 of these . . . Don't count the balloons!

Hint: the hippo did!

Some of the animals have found it too! Which animals are they?

5 of these . . .